In loving memory of my mother who
blessed me, for my grandmother who continues
to bless me, and for Tyrel, Tierra and Talon
who are a blessing.

- Brenda

To every child who has been blessed with the
wisdom of their grandma's stories, advice, and love.

- Trisha

Bella's Blessings

WRITTEN BY *Brenda Stokes*

ILLUSTRATIONS BY *Trisha DesRosiers*

Bella Beaver was born on a sunny spring morning. Grandma Beaver looked down at her tiny grandkit and felt like her heart was bursting, it was so full of love. Suddenly, Grandma Beaver knew just what she had to do.

Grandma Beaver took the blanket that hung on her rocking chair and then she found the old blanket that she had wrapped all her baby kits in many years ago. She carefully cut a piece of material from the corner of each blanket. She sat in her rocking chair and sewed the two pieces into a blessing bag. As Grandma Beaver rocked and sewed, she thought about her many blessings and smiled. When she was done, she sewed Bella's name on the front.

Grandma Beaver swam out of the beaver lodge and over to the riverbank to find a special stone. As she looked at the many different stones, she saw a small green caterpillar inch itself off a smooth round one. Grandma Beaver picked up the stone and it felt just right in her paw. She quickly swam back with it to the lodge.

She wrote 'Love' on the stone and put it into the blessing bag. She picked up Bella, gave her a gentle beaver hug, and said, "I am so blessed to have you as my grandkit. In return I shall bless you each spring. Bella Beaver, this spring I bless you with love. Know that I love you wherever you are and may you pass this love on to others."

Grandma Beaver kissed Bella on the forehead and Bella let out a happy giggle.

As Bella grew that year, she was bursting with *love*! She smiled and giggled and made all the animals around her feel loved.

Grouchy Mr. Muskrat thought kits were too loud and too pesky. Most kits stayed out of his way.

But not Bella! She smiled and waved every time she saw grouchy old Mr. Muskrat. And if Mr. Muskrat was sure that no one else was looking, he would smile and wink back at her.

The next spring, Grandma Beaver wrote 'Dedication' on a special stone and put it into Bella's blessing bag. She picked up Bella, gave her a great big beaver hug, and said, "Bella Beaver, every moment I spend with you is a blessing. In return I shall bless you with *dedication*. May you face new challenges with hard work." Grandma Beaver gently kissed Bella on the forehead.

Bella smiled. "I love you, Grandma Beaver!"

Bella loved to dance. She danced around her lodge. She danced along the riverbank. She danced in the forest, and she even danced in her bed! One day, when Bella was dancing down the path, she saw a sign that read:

**BEAVER HOP LESSONS
5 P.M. WEDNESDAYS
COMMUNITY LODGE**

Bella was so excited that she ran, not danced, all the way home to tell Mama Beaver the exciting news. Mama Beaver signed her up for the lessons right away.

Bella was thrilled to be taking real beaver hop dance lessons. The class was full of other animals who also loved to dance. Many of them were very good. Bella liked the lessons, but she found some of the steps quite tricky.

Papa Beaver could see that Bella was getting frustrated. "Bella Beaver, remember that you've been blessed with *dedication*. Is there a way you could enjoy your lessons without worrying?"

Bella thought for a while and then she said, "Maybe if I practiced everyday, I'd be ready for the next lesson."

So Bella did just that. She practiced and practiced until her paws hurt. On the night of the recital, Bella moved her paws in perfect time to the music.

Bella felt like a star!

Bella grew quickly and before anyone knew it, another spring had arrived. Grandma Beaver wrote 'Honesty' on a special stone and put it into Bella's blessing bag.

She gave Bella a great big beaver hug and said, "Bella Beaver, I have been so blessed to watch you dance and grow. In return I shall bless you with honesty. May you always tell the truth and be a beaver others can trust." Grandma Beaver kissed Bella on the forehead and Bella beamed back at her.

The only thing Bella liked more than her adventures was telling Papa Beaver about them. One day, when Papa Beaver asked Bella if she had done anything exciting that day, she couldn't think of a single thing, so she blurted out, "I caught fifteen butterflies in my net, but one of them bit me with its teeth and they all got away." As soon as the words flew out of her mouth, Bella got a bad feeling in her tummy. She knew it had something to do with her *honesty* blessing.

Papa Beaver looked disappointed as he said, "Bella, I'm quite sure butterflies do not have teeth."

Bella went to bed early that night, but she didn't sleep well.

The next morning, Bella knew she needed to make things right.

"Papa Beaver, when I told you about the butterflies, well, that wasn't actually the truth," Bella confessed.

Papa Beaver smiled and replied, "I didn't think so, Bella. It made me feel sad when you lied."

"I'm sorry, Papa Beaver," Bella said as she hugged him. "From now on, I'll remember my *honesty* blessing."

Bella's tummy felt much better so she ate a huge breakfast!

Another spring arrived and Bella was excited just thinking about her next blessing. Grandma Beaver wrote 'Beauty' on a special stone and put it into Bella's blessing bag. She hugged Bella and said, "Bella Beaver, I am so blessed by the joy you have brought into my life. In return I shall bless you. May you see the *beauty* in all that is around you and may you share this beauty with others."

Grandma Beaver leaned over and kissed Bella on the forehead. "Thank you, Grandma," said Bella.

The next morning, Bella got up bright and early. In one corner of the lodge, she spied a spider spinning a web.

Bella was just about to yell, "Papa! Help! There's a spider!" when she remembered her *beauty* blessing.

So instead, Bella watched the spider spin each delicate thread. She couldn't help but notice what a beautiful web it was making.

One lazy summer afternoon, Bella and her friends floated on their backs in the river. "Look, there's a castle!" Bella said as she pointed at a fluffy white cloud in the sky.

Soon Bella's friends were pointing out clouds shaped like trains, dinosaurs, and even flying elephants. They giggled as they took in the beauty of the sky. Bella's *beauty* blessing had come true.

Another year passed and Bella began to wonder what her blessing would be this spring. Bella found Grandma Beaver rocking quietly in her chair. Grandma Beaver held out a special stone that read 'Kindness'.

Bella slipped the stone into her blessing bag and then Grandma Beaver said, "Bella Beaver, I have been so blessed to watch you fulfill your blessings. In return I shall bless you with kindness. When someone is sad or feeling left out, may you reach out with a kind heart, kind words, and kind actions."

Then Grandma Beaver leaned over and kissed Bella on the cheek. Bella kissed her back.

Bella loved going to school. One morning, Bella's teacher, Mrs. Loon, made a big announcement: "Class, I'd like you to meet our new student, Peggy Porcupine."

Peggy Porcupine's cheeks went red and she barely took her eyes off the ground. Bella was sure that Peggy Porcupine needed a friend so she set out to put her *kindness* blessing into action. At recess, Bella skipped right over to Peggy Porcupine and asked her if she'd like to play a game of hopscotch.

"Hopscotch is for babies!" Peggy sneered.

"Would you like to play something else then?" Bella asked.

"Just leave me alone," Peggy said as she stormed away.

Bella didn't know what to do. That night she told Mama Beaver what had happened.

Mama Beaver listened patiently and then said, "Sometimes classmates act mean to cover up their real feelings. Just give Peggy time."

So, everyday Bella invited Peggy to play, but everyday Peggy refused and scowled at Bella.

One afternoon, Bella found Peggy Porcupine up in a tree, crying.

"Can I help you?" Bella called up to Peggy.

For the first time, Peggy didn't say anything mean.

"I've moved far away from my dad, my old den, and all my friends.
I was mad at first but now I'm just lonely," sniffed Peggy.

Bella reached for Peggy's prickly paw and led her to the playground.
Bella's *kindness* blessing was finally working.

Things were changing for Bella. Grandma Beaver was sick a lot. Some days she couldn't even get out of bed, but she was always happy to see Bella.

Sometimes they would talk, sometimes Grandma Beaver would show Bella how to sew, and sometimes Bella would read to Grandma Beaver.

One evening, Papa Beaver proudly announced, "Bella, next spring you are going to be a big sister."

Bella was thrilled! She hugged her parents and danced around the room. That night, Bella dreamed about all the fun she would have with her little brother or sister kit.

By the time spring arrived, Grandma Beaver rarely rose from her bed. One sunny afternoon, Bella sat and softly sang one of Grandma Beaver's favorite songs to her. Grandma Beaver opened her eyes and looked up at Bella with so much love. Slowly, Grandma Beaver opened her paw and revealed a blessing stone that read 'Courage'.

Her voice whispered, "Thank you, Bella, for being such a blessing in my life. I bless you with courage. May you remember all your blessings and take courage … " And then Grandma Beaver closed her eyes.

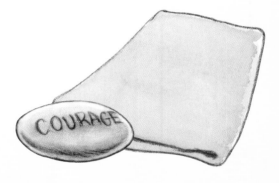

Grandma Beaver never did finish telling Bella the rest of her *courage* blessing, and in the long days that followed, Grandma Beaver never did open her eyes again.

Bella missed her Grandma Beaver so much. But Grandma Beaver and her blessings had a way of showing up. One sunny afternoon, Bella smiled when she noticed Grandma's favorite flowers in bloom, which reminded her of her *beauty* blessing. Another day, when Bella forgot her school lunch, Peggy shared with her – her *kindness* blessing. Grandma Beaver's blessings were with Bella wherever she went.

Slowly, Bella started to feel her *courage* blessing. At last she understood. Bella needed to take courage from all her blessings and not be so sad. As long as she remembered her blessings, Grandma Beaver would always be with her.

"Come and meet Benjamin Beaver, your new baby brother!" Papa Beaver happily announced as he woke Bella early one morning.

When Bella looked down at her little brother, she felt like her heart was bursting, it was so full of love. Suddenly, Bella knew just what she had to do.

Bella took the blanket that lay on her own bed and then she found the old blanket that Grandma Beaver had used when she sat in her rocking chair. Bella carefully cut off a piece of material from each blanket. She sat in Grandma Beaver's rocking chair and sewed the two pieces into a blessing bag. As Bella rocked and sewed, she thought about her many blessings and smiled. When she was done, she sewed Benjamin's name on the front.

Bella swam out of the beaver lodge and over to the riverbank to find a special stone. As she looked around at the many stones, a beautiful butterfly landed on a smooth round one. The butterfly flew away and Bella picked up the stone. It felt just right in her paw. She quickly swam back with it to the lodge.

Bella wrote 'Love' on the stone and put it into the blessing bag. She picked up Benjamin, gave him a gentle beaver hug, and said, "I am so blessed to have you as my little brother kit. In return I shall bless you each spring. Benjamin Beaver, this spring I bless you with love. May you feel Grandma Beaver's love even though you'll never meet her. May you always know the love of your family and love us back."

Then Bella kissed Benjamin on the forehead and Benjamin let out a happy giggle.

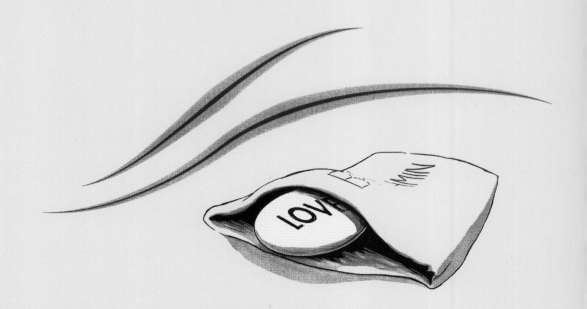

Published in 2012 by Simply Read Books www.simplyreadbooks.com
Text © 2012 Brenda Stokes · Illustrations © 2012 Trisha DesRosiers

Library and Archives Canada Cataloguing in Publication

Stokes, Brenda, 1969–
Bella's blessings / written by Brenda Stokes : illustrated by Trisha DesRosiers.
ISBN 978-1-897476-61-1
I.DesRosiers, Trisha II. Title.
S8637.T647B45 2011   JC813'.6   C2011-900528-X

We gratefully acknowledge for their financial support of our publishing program the Canada Council for the Arts, the BC Arts
Council, and the Government of Canada through the Canada Book Fund (CBF).

Manufactured in Singapore

10 9 8 7 6 5 4 3 2 1